The Sweet Touch

Lorna and Lecia Balian

Star Bright Books
New York

Published in the United States of America by Star Bright Books, Inc., New York.
The name Star Bright Books and the Star Bright Books logo are registered trademarks of Star Bright Books, Inc. Please visit www.starbrightbooks.com.

ISBN 1-59572-017-0

Printed in China 9 8 7 6 5 4 3 2 1

Library of Congress Cataloging-in-Publication Data

Balian, Lorna.
  The sweet touch / by Lorna and Lecia Balian.
      p. cm.
  Summary: The genie conjured up by Peggy's plastic ring is only a beginner who does not know how to put a stop to the one wish he can grant.
  ISBN 1-59572-017-0
  [1. Genies--Fiction. 2. Magic--Fiction.] I. Balian, Lecia. II. Title.

PZ7.B1978Sw 2005
[E]--dc22
                                                    2004029603

for Peggy and Penny. . .

Peggy found a penny.
She put the penny into
a nearby gumball machine,
but instead of a gumball,
a shiny, genuine plastic, gold
ring rolled into her hand.

Peggy liked the ring
well enough, but she
was very fond of
sweets and would
have preferred a
cherry gumball.

She put the ring on her finger
and wandered off, hoping to
find another penny.

When Peggy was tucked into bed for the night
she remembered the shiny, genuine plastic, gold
ring. She turned it around on her finger and
rubbed it to see if the shiny would come off. . .

. . . the BED TREMBLED,
and out of a puff of smelly dust,
a strange, tiny creature appeared.

Peggy yanked the quilt over her head
and huddled with her eyes scrunched
shut and her heart pounding.

"Silly girl," a wee voice whispered in
her ear. "I won't hurt you."

Peggy peeked at him.
"Who are you?" she asked timidly.
"I am Oliver, The Magnificent
Magic Genie."

He looked so funny and sounded so funny that Peggy started to giggle. Oliver was indignant! He said he had come to grant her one magic wish, and he certainly wasn't going to do it if she was going to laugh at him.

Peggy stopped giggling and looked at Oliver doubtfully.
"If you are a really, truly, magic genie, why can't I
have three magic wishes like everybody else?"

Oliver said, "I am only a tiny genie and rather new at
the magic business. I can only manage one wish."

Well, one wish is better than none,
but it's a difficult thing to decide.
So they sat down to think it over.

Peggy thought it would be lovely
if she could have a big chunk of
creamy chocolate fudge.

Oliver said, "Peppermint sticks might
be better. Red spots pop out all over
me whenever I eat chocolate."

Peggy thought a barrel of gumdrops
would be nice. "A truckload of
candied cherries would be even better!"

"A lollipop tree?"

"Gallons and gallons of root beer!"

"Five hundred ice-cream cones—all flavors!"

"A million jelly beans?"

"Wait!" said Oliver, "I know just what to do. I'll give you the MAGIC TOUCH!" He explained to Peggy that it was not easy to do, but if he could manage it, everything she touched would turn into something sweet.

Peggy agreed that it would be the best way to get everything they wanted with just one wish, so she said:

"I WISH EVERYTHING I TOUCH WOULD TURN INTO SOMETHING SWEET!"

Oliver stood on his head and rubbed his wings together.

He wiggled his toes, licked his fingers, and jumped up and down six times.

He whispered some magic words into his pocket, flew around Peggy's head seventy-three times, and sat down to say the alphabet backwards.

Suddenly, they were surrounded
by the sweet smell of chocolate.
"I've done it! I've done it!" whooped Oliver.
"Your feet! Look at your feet!"

The rug under Peggy's feet had turned into
soft, gooey chocolate, and it was squishing
up between her toes.

Peggy happily licked her toes.
"Touch something else," Oliver begged.
"You know I can't eat chocolate."

Peggy plopped around her room leaving a gooey chocolate trail and touching everything in sight.

Her jump rope became a licorice whip.

The bedposts turned to gingerbread.

Her new crayons became candy sticks.
Marbles turned into jawbreakers and bubblegum balls.
And her very best beads became a necklace of jelly beans.

They nibbled and giggled and ate and ate.

Peggy jumped on the bed and sank into
a very soft marshmallow mattress.

Her pillowcase changed to fine spun sugar,
which quickly tore, and feathers billowed
out as cotton candy.

"My quilt has turned to taffy, Oliver!"
shrieked Peggy. "Help me pull it!"

Peggy took one corner of the quilt,
Oliver took another,
and they pulled and tugged
and twisted the tacky stuff
until they were so tangled up
they could barely move.

"Oliver, I have a tummy ache," said Peggy.
"I think you'd better turn the wish off now."

"I haven't learned how to do that yet. I only
know how to turn a wish on," said Oliver sadly.

"I'm tired and thirsty," wailed Peggy,
syrupy tears rolling down her face.

"Me too," said Oliver, "and I want to go home,
but I can't fly with all this taffy on my wings."

"What are we going to do?" Peggy asked him.

"Well, let me think about it," said Oliver.

And he thought. . .

and he thought. . .

and he thought. . .
and he thought. . .

and he thought.

They were both sound asleep when
Oliver's mother flitted into the room.
She had been looking for Oliver all night!

"My, my! What a mess!" she muttered softly.
"What am I going to do with that boy?"

She pried him loose from the tangle of taffy and scraped the marshmallow from his bottom.

She propped him up and wiggled him until he sleepily muttered the alphabet–frontwards.

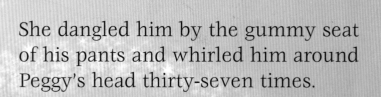

She dangled him by the gummy seat of his pants and whirled him around Peggy's head thirty-seven times.

She emptied the magic
words out of his pocket.

She jumped down and
up with him six times.

She cleaned off
his fingers with the
hem of her petticoat
and untangled his
sticky wings.

She turned him over her knees,
gave him a love-pat on the fanny,

a kiss on the nose,

and carried him off into the sunrise.

Peggy woke up with her quilt all twisted and tangled around her and feathers stuck in her hair. She looked at the shiny, genuine plastic, gold ring on her finger and wondered if the shiny would come off if she rubbed on it. . .